Sensation

The Emmaus Grail

By

David J H Smith

AMAZON EDITION

Paige Croft Publishing, Yeovil, Somerset

David J H Smith asserts the moral right to be identified as the author of this work

Cover Template by Jo Stroud
Cover Art 'The Emmaus Grail' by Jo Stroud

Amazon Edition - 2021

Published by Paige Croft Publishing
Printed through Amazon

Also available on Amazon Kindle

All rights reserved. No part of this publication may be reproduced, stored in a retrieval system, or transmitted, in any form or by any means: electronic, mechanical, photocopying, recording or otherwise, without the prior permission of the publisher.

This book is sold subject to the condition that it shall not, by way of trade or otherwise, be lent, re-sold, hired out or otherwise circulated without the authors prior consent in any form or binding other than that in which it is published and without a similar condition including this condition being imposed on the subsequent purchaser

Sensational Tales
The Emmaus Grail

About the author

David J H Smith was originally from Slough, Berkshire but is now living in Somerset.

He graduated from Thames Valley University with an Honours Degree in History & Geography before going on to study History at Post Graduate level at Westminster University.

David has worked in various jobs such as Immigration, Retail Manager, Facilities Officer and IT before becoming a writer and setting up 'Things From Dimension - X' which specialises in the sale of rare and collectable comic books.

Other Works:

The Titanic's Mummy

CHAPTER 1

Miss Owl and The Wasp took on heroic poses while the female partygoer, who had stopped them in the street, got out her phone and started to take photos of them.

The Wasp was dressed in a grey suit with a red shirt and thick black tie, which was partially hidden by a bright red cape that went down to his knees. On his head, over his dark hair, he wore a matching red fedora hat that had a black ribbon around its base. Over his eyes he wore a simple black strip of cloth with two holes cut into it to allow him to see.

Miss Owl was dressed in a blue sleeveless top and blue shorts with matching blue ankle boots. She wore a blue cowl over her face and blonde hair that was connected to a long cape- under which was a large brown canvas satchel.

After a few moments the flashes from the camera phone stopped and, after checking her screen, the girl looked up and smiled. "Thank you so much!" she said happily.

"No problem," replied The Wasp, as he relaxed his pose.

"So where's Blue Bolt and Firefly?" asked the girl, looking around the busy town centre which was lit by street lights and the light of what was left of the moon. "I was hoping to meet all of you 'Guardians'."

"Oh, they won't be far," replied Miss Owl, as she reached into her satchel and produced a pair of pink flip flops. "Here, take these. I have a feeling you'll be needing them by the end of the night judging by the height of those heels."

"Thank you," replied the girl, with a smile, "you guys are awesome. What you do is amazing." She then turned and headed off to re-join the group of friends who were waiting for her.

Miss Owl (Lucy Randell, who was 19 years old), The Wasp (Glenn Keats, 22), Blue Bolt (Carl Wallace, 20) and Firefly (Will Hines, 24) were collectively known as 'The Guardians'. They patrolled the town centre every Friday and Saturday night. Their self-appointed task was to ensure those who were enjoying an evening out were safe and, if they spotted any trouble, to alert the authorities. Each carried a First Aid Kit which they were trained in using, as well as other useful items such as flip flops, bottles of water and disposable rain coverings that could be given out as required.

The whole idea was the brainchild of Glenn, and he soon enlisted the help of his three friends in the venture. Partly as they genuinely wanted to help people, but also as it gave them a chance to don the costumes of their favourite superheroes from days gone by, taking them from the pages of comic books to real life.

The four were now familiar figures around the town and had even gained a small amount of fame: with some of their exploits being reported in the local papers, and of course on social media.

As well as their nightly patrols they also attended school fetes, made visits to the children's ward and homes for the elderly. They also took part in fundraising events for local charities and hospices, and last year they were even invited to turn on the town's Christmas lights.

Although largely accepted as a positive, the local police did treat them warily and with caution. "We don't mind you going out on your patrols and helping people," Sargent Singh had once told them, "but there is a fine line between this and overstepping into official police business. I don't want any of you to make the leap to becoming vigilantes and take things into your own hands.

More importantly, I certainly don't want to see you end up getting yourselves hurt." The Guardians took on what was said and ensured that they did not overstep that line or interfere with any police activity.

Suddenly a thought struck Miss Owl. "Hey, that's a point. Where *are* Firefly and Blue Bolt? Shouldn't they have checked in with us by now?"

"Yes, actually you're right, they should have," observed The Wasp as he pulled out his mobile phone from his jacket pocket.

As well as patrolling in twos, for safety, they had made it a policy to regularly communicate with each other and mobile phones were the perfect device. Not just in terms of calls and texts, but it had allowed them to download a tracing app so they could keep track of each other's exact location.

The Wasp looked down at the phone and shrugged. "No messages but, from the app, they seem to be heading back to base."

"A bit early for a break isn't it?" pondered Miss Owl. "It's not even 9.30pm."

Then from nearby there was a scream.

Turning round Miss Owl and The Wasp could see the cry had come from 'Mario's Takeaway Pizza' place.

The patrons had run out of the building, the door slowly closing behind them, inadvertently shutting in the cause of their alarm - a large red fox who, drawn by the chance of food, had brazenly wandered inside. Visible through the large plate glass window the three members of staff, who were behind the counter which ran right across the building, could be seen shouting and trying to scare the fox. But these actions only seemed to alarm the creature even further.

Miss Owl and The Wasp instantly responded by running over to the takeaway. The Wasp opened the door hoping that the fox seeing its chance for freedom, would take it. However, the creature, seemingly confused, ignored the escape route and withdrew further back into the building; into the far corner of the counter which met the wall.

"I'm going to take a more direct approach," said The Wasp, as he moved into the building. Miss Owl went to the door, holding it open. By now one of the workers in the shop had moved forward and had lifted the hinged top of the counter. He was about to open the small gate-like door it hid, but The Wasp stopped him. "No it's okay, I've got this."

The takeaway worker immediately backed off.

"Can you get me a broom, mop or something?" The Wasp asked.

The man nodded, disappearing off and returning moments later with a large wooden broom which he passed over the counter to The Wasp. He grabbed hold of it and then, holding the brush end out in front of him, slowly circled the big glass window making his way over to the fox.

"Careful!" warned Miss Owl, "cornered animals are always at their most dangerous."

"It's alright," cried The Wasp, as he drew level with the fox that was watching him intently and then starting to quietly snarl. "I've got it, just keep that door open and stand clear." Slowly and carefully he reached out with the broom. At first he thought the animal was going to attack, but then the fox made a run for it and ran across the takeaway to the open door and out into the street where it ran off, disappearing into the night.

Then, from the disturbed patrons of the shop and those inside who worked there, a cheer went up for Miss Owl and The Wasp and their heroics.

"Thank you! Thank you!" said Mario, the owner of the takeaway. "That could have been nasty: if that creature had bitten anyone, oh my goodness!"

"That's alright," replied The Wasp, "glad to be of help."

Mario turned to one of his employees. "Giuseppe, go and take the broom, then get the mop and bucket. We need to clean the floor before we can have any customers back in."

He then turned back to The Wasp and Miss Owl. "Right, for you, two large pizzas to show my thanks."

"Thank you," replied The Wasp, "but there is really no need." However, the sight and smell of two pizzas on the grill caught his attention. "Although, well, we haven't actually eaten yet, and we know how good your pizzas are so …"

CHAPTER 2

Not wanting to let their pizzas go cold, and aware that Firefly and Blue Bolt had already gone back to their headquarters, The Wasp and Miss Owl decided to join them so they could all eat the food together.

The place that served as their almost secret base could not have been more fitting for The Guardians; bearing in mind they based themselves on superheroes. 'Starfire Comics & Action Figures' was owned by Jon Goldman who, after hearing what the group were doing, quickly made contact with them and offered them the use of his staff room above the shop. The shop opened late into the evening every Friday and Saturday which tied in perfectly with their patrols. The facilities there gave them a place to change, take comfort breaks and chill out.

As The Wasp and Miss Owl approached, Jon appeared in the doorway with a look of worry and concern on his face. "Glenn, Lucy, come quick!" he called, as he beckoned them to hurry. "There's been an accident, Carl's been injured!"

"How bad?" asked Glenn.

"He's bruised and shaken. Come and see for yourself," replied Jon, as they hurried to the shop where he took them through the people, seated at tables playing various board and card games, to the back of the building and a door marked 'Staff Only' which took them up a small flight of stairs to the first floor and the area that 'The Guardians' used. And there, sitting at a small table looking slightly stunned and sorry for himself, holding a wet towel to his head half covering his brown hair, was Carl aka 'Blue Bolt' who was dressed in a blue body suit with a long cape and matching boots. Embossed on his chest was a large yellow lightning bolt while, lying on the table, was his blue skull-cap along with his equipment satchel.

Standing over him, looking worried, was Will aka Firefly. His costume consisted of a black cotton onesie, which showed off his muscular physique, over which he wore red shorts and just above that his equipment belt. On his feet he wore red boots which went up to his knees and on his hands he had matching red gauntlets. Tied around his head, over his dark hair, he normally wore a thin piece of black cloth with eye holes in them, but he had taken this off and tucked it in to his belt.

"Are you alright?" asked Glenn worriedly, as he and Lucy moved over to them, placing the pizza down on the table.

"A slightly twisted ankle and a few bumps and bruises mainly; nothing too serious, although he could have been worse," Will replied.

"What happened?" asked Lucy.

"Well we were on patrol at the top end of town," started Carl, "when I thought I saw a light coming from one of the old cottages behind St Mary's church. So we decided to go and investigate."

"Carl!" said Glenn disapprovingly, "you know you shouldn't be going there! That place is off limits!"

"I know," replied Carl apologetically, "but we weren't planning to go right up to the cottages themselves. We just sort of took a look from the edge of things. If we spotted anything amiss we were going to call the police straight away and let them handle things."

At the top of the main high street, off to one side, there was a large medieval church surrounded by a substantial graveyard; with graves dating back to the early 1600's. At the back of the church, on the edge of its land boundary, was a row of boarded up cottages. The ownership of these empty buildings had been in dispute for decades. The church saying they belonged to them as they were on their land, while a firm of local solicitors said that they were theirs, claiming them as part of an estate that had reverted to them. As the wrangling went on, the four cottages fell into disrepair. Neither side were willing to let the other take responsibility for their upkeep, as this could be seen as a claim of ownership, while unwilling to pay out for it themselves. At one point squatters entered one of the buildings and set up home, but eventually left causing major damage. It was at this point that the local historical society got involved and tried to take out a court order to get them protected and listed as special historical interest with claims there were links to Lord Wellington, but failed. Then, seeing the trouble the cottages were causing and the state of them, the local council were forced to intervene. They sent in a team to board up all the doors and windows in case any further damage could happen to them.

Due to the fact the churchyard sometimes attracted some of the more undesirable elements of society because of its secluded location, it had been decided that the Guardians would go nowhere near it on their patrols for their own safety.

"Anyway," continued Carl, "we were making our way through the old gravestones when I stumbled in the dark; my foot went into one of the sunken graves and threw me off-balance and I went over. As I fell I ended up hitting my head on one of the old headstones." He lifted the towel to reveal a large bruise on his forehead.

"Ouch!" exclaimed Lucy, looking at the injury, "that looks nasty."

"It's okay," replied Will quickly, "I've already checked him over thoroughly, no signs of concussion. It looks a lot worse than it is." He gave a quick smile. "Luckily it was only his head and nothing important that he injured."

"Yes, thanks for that," replied Carl, trying to overlook the friendly jibe, "anyway," he continued, "after my little mishap we decided to come back here."

"Looks like you two had the same idea," accused Will, looking down at the pizzas. "You weren't planning on taking a sneaky supper break without letting us know, were you?"

"No, far from it," replied Glenn with a smile, as he went to open the box and offered it to them, "we saw you were here on the app so decided to come and share. Come on guys dig in." And with that he and Miss Owl went on to tell of their little adventure at the pizza shop with the Fox, as they shared out the pizza.

"You know," said Will thoughtfully," I've noticed them getting bolder and bolder. We need to make a real effort in picking up rubbish and putting it in the bins. After all, that's what's attracting them."

"Or why not go further and turn it into an event?" suggested Glenn. "A litter pick, perhaps even get the press involved? We could get the Scouts and Girl Guides to participate."

The four continued to discuss the idea until the pizza was finished and then decided to call it a night. The small group quickly updated the group's social media and then changed out of their costumes into their normal clothes and headed downstairs into the shop. There they first confirmed with Jon that Carl was alright, if a little battered, before joining the rest of the patrons in the remainder of the Games Night.

At 11pm Jon made his announcement that the shop would be closing in half an hour, which gave those in the shop a chance to finish off their games and to pack up. The Guardians quickly put their game away and, as they normally did, helped Jon with the tidying up and the shutting up of the shop, once the last customers had left.

Then, with the alarm set and security shutter closed, Glenn offered to give Carl a lift home to save him walking and to make sure he got back safely, which was readily accepted. With that they said their goodbyes and they all headed off home.

CHAPTER 3

Glenn, Lucy and Will met as normal the following evening at the comic shop just before 8.00pm. During the day they had all called to check how Carl was doing and, although feeling much better, he had decided to give tonight's patrol a miss, which under the circumstances they totally understood.

After the remaining Guardians had changed into their superhero costumes and checked their equipment, they headed out for their nightly patrol as a trio. As they neared St Mary's church, The

Wasp stopped and found himself staring into the graveyard and to the old cottages.

"Hey, what's up?" asked Miss Owl.

"Something just occurred to me," he replied, before turning to Firefly, "with everything that went on last night with Blue Bolt, we forgot to ask. That light you thought you saw, did you work out what it was?"

Firefly shook his head. "No, Blue Bolt took his tumble pretty much as soon as we started to take a look, and then I took him straight back to base, so we didn't get a chance to investigate properly."

The Wasp looked back into the graveyard intently.

"You think we should investigate?" asked Firefly.

The Wasp nodded.

"Are you sure?" asked Miss Owl. "You were the one who said that we shouldn't go there."

"I know," replied The Wasp, "but I think just this once. Just in case there is something amiss.

Which house was it you thought you saw the light?"

"The last one on the right," replied Firefly, "we thought we saw a glow by the front door."

"Alright," said The Wasp, "let's go and take a quick look."

The three of them crossed the road and headed towards the church's open lych gate, which they passed through entering into the graveyard. They first of all moved down the main path that led towards the church's door. Then, they stepped off the path, heading down the right hand side of the building, carefully walking through the graves to the back of the graveyard to where the abandoned cottages were located. Once there they stopped outside the waist high iron railing fence which separated the small row of four buildings from the graveyard itself.

The four small cottages, which must have been at least a hundred years old, were built out of a light grey stone brick, which matched that of the main church. On the roof were light terracotta tiles, a number of which had slipped out of place or were missing altogether. All of the windows and doors had been covered by grey protective metal grilles to prevent anyone breaking in.

"Well," said Miss Owl, casting her eye over the buildings, "seems totally deserted and there's certainly no light here now."

"But that doesn't mean to say that there wasn't one yesterday," pointed out The Wasp.

He then moved to the gap in the railing, where a gate should have stood, and walked into the cottage's grounds with Miss Owl and Firefly following. Through the uneven ground they made for the last house on the right where they stopped to take a closer look.

"Well, all the grating's intact and hasn't been tampered with," noted Firefly.

"The front of the cottage, yes," replied The Wasp, "but remember there would be a back door too."

"That would make sense," speculated Miss Owl, "if anyone was breaking in they would be out of sight."

The three then moved to the side of the cottage and followed the building round until they found themselves at the back on a long strip of communal ground which once served as a backyard area. Straight away they could see that the large grating that covered the back door of the last cottage had been tampered with. The grating's security screws which held it in place had been removed and the metal sheet itself was leaning at a slight angle over the cottage's door.

"Someone's been here alright," said Firefly.

"Yes," agreed The Wasp, inspecting the grill, "and for them to remove those security screws properly and not force it I don't think we are looking at kids or those with addiction issues. You need special tools to do that and they are not easily available for obvious security reasons."

"We should really call this in," said Miss Owl, "notify the Police and let them deal with it from here."

"I'd like to take a bit more of a look first," said Firefly. "If the grating's been moved, the door's bound to be open. Let's take a look inside."

"I'm totally sure we shouldn't," warned Miss Owl. "Aside from the fact we've no idea what could be in there, we could get into trouble for trespassing."

"Just a quick peek," insisted Firefly. "That way we can give the police a real picture as to what's going on."

The Wasp paused then nodded. "Alright, I guess that couldn't hurt."

Firefly moved in towards the door. Taking the grating in both hands he moved it over slightly and then cautiously peered through the gap that he had created.

"Well?" asked The Wasp, "anything?"

Firefly slowly nodded. "Well, the original door has been completely removed. There's something going on here alright." He then moved back and again took hold of the grating. This time he moved it completely to reveal the opening going directly into the kitchen and, before anyone could stop him, he stepped inside.

"What are you doing?" hissed The Wasp. He looked over at Miss Owl, shaking his head, and then followed Firefly inside. With a sigh, Miss Owl followed, and the three found themselves inside a small kitchen.

The room was dully lit by a number of battery operated strip lights that had strategically been stuck on the walls. A small fold out camping table had been placed in the middle of the floor around which were four chairs. The small Belfast sink was filled with full plastic water bottles. Nearby, on the counter, were bags of shopping. On the floor, in the space where a fridge would have been, was a large portable cooler and in the space where an oven would have stood was a camping stove connected to a small gas cylinder. Placed on the counter immediately to the right was a selection of unwashed mugs next to a jar of coffee and an open bag of sugar.

"I think it's safe to say this place is being used by someone," observed The Wasp, in a quiet voice, "and by the looks of the way things are set up they have been here for a while."

"Yes," agreed Firefly, "this certainly explains the light that we saw last night."

"Come on," insisted The Wasp, "the mystery is solved. Let's go before whoever is squatting realises we are here. We can make a report to the police tomorrow and let them deal with it from there."

"Hold on," said Miss Owl, seeing something in the far corner of the room, "what are those sacks for?" She pointed to a large pile of about thirty neatly folded industrial strength refuse bags.

"Well spotted," said The Wasp, "you certainly live up to your name with that great eyesight and observational skills!"

"Thank you," she replied, smiling, "so what do you think?"

"Dunno," said Firefly, with a shrug, "perhaps they're there so they can tidy up after themselves?"

"Well they're not doing a good job," replied Miss Owl, looking around at the state the kitchen was in, "and why the heavy duty variety? No it has to be for something else." Her eyes drifted around the room to the door which led into another room, from which a similar dim light, presumably from more battery operated lights, was emulating. She turned to The Wasp. "Well? What do you say?"

After a short pause The Wasp, his interest caught, nodded. The three of them headed over to the door which led directly into the cottage's sitting room.

CHAPTER 4

Two things were immediately noticeable as they entered the room. Firstly part of one wall had crudely been knocked through to give access to the next door cottage, and secondly the room was filled with sacks like those they had just found in the kitchen. However, these ones were full.

The Wasp moved over to one of them, opened it up and looked inside.

"Well?" asked Miss Owl eagerly.

"Earth," he replied, as he picked up a handful of soil, which had a mustard tinge to it, and let it slip through his fingers back into the sack. He moved to another and opened it and looked inside, and then to a third. "Yes," he confirmed, "so are these. They must all be filled with soil."

"There must be tonnes of it here," said Firefly, looking at all the sacks stacked up, "but why?"

"Come on," said The Wasp, looking at the hole in the wall leading to the next cottage's lounge, where again a dull light was emanating, "let's take a look." He then moved over to the opening and stepped in, followed by Miss Owl and Firefly. The three of them found themselves in a scene from a cheap horror movie.

On a large fold out table, carefully laid out, was a skeleton which looked to be that of an adult.

Leaning up against one wall were three new cheap looking coffins and just by them was a pile of what looked like shrouds and next to that a stack of old clothes.

Again, like they had seen before, a section of one wall had been knocked down allowing access directly into the next cottage.

One word that summed up the scene and what was going on in these cottages sprang to mind. It was Miss Owl who voiced it out loud. "Body Snatchers! They are digging underneath the graveyard and harvesting the old skeletons."

"Yeah, that's it," said The Wasp, nodding, "that's the only explanation."

"But hold on a moment," replied Firefly, slightly confused, "grave robbing went on hundreds of years ago. It was when bodies that had just been buried were stolen and sold to Doctors and Surgeons so they can see how the body worked. They didn't dig up old skeletons."

"I know," said The Wasp thoughtfully, "this is something different, and I have a bad feeling I know what." From his pocket he then produced his phone and started to look something up. "Yes, it's as I thought," he said after a short while, "there are websites that sell real antique human remains and they go for big money."

"Really?" asked Miss Owl, "how much?"

"£6000 for a full male skeleton, £350 for an adult skull with a full set of teeth, £150 for a complete hand or foot, the list goes on," replied The Wasp.

"Wow!" exclaimed Firefly in surprise. "The remains in this graveyard must be worth thousands upon thousands."

"And not just that," commented Miss Owl, looking at the small pile of clothes by the shrouds, "those suits, dresses and the like would be worth a fortune on the vintage clothes scene, not to mention anything else that might have been buried with them such as jewellery and bibles."

"Who would want to buy clothes someone's been buried in?" asked Firefly in disgust.

"I'm not sure that would be a key selling feature," quipped The Wasp, "although that said, bearing in mind people seem happy to buy human remains, I'm actually not so sure!"

"C'mon," said Firefly looking at the hole in the wall which led into the next house where a now familiar glow was coming through, "we've come this far."

The Wasp nodded and the three moved across the room and through the opening where they found themselves in the sitting room of the third house.

Stacked around the side of the room were more bags filled with earth that had been excavated from the graveyard. On the wall just by them was what looked to be a plan of the churchyard, which was no doubt used to locate the graves, underneath that were a number of spades and pickaxes. In the middle of the floor was a large hole, over which was a pulley and rope system connected to the ceiling, used for hauling up full sacks of excavated earth. Moving over to the hole and looking down into it, the Guardians could see a wooden ladder attached to the side as well as a string of lights.

"That looks pretty deep," noted Firefly.

"Bodies are buried six feet underground," said Miss Owl, "they would have to dig down even further to get access to the graves. I would guess there is a whole network of tunnels down there."

"There's only one way to find out," said The Wasp, as he moved closer to the hole and started to manoeuvre himself onto the ladder and down into the shaft. Firefly followed with Miss Owl not far behind, and the three of them found themselves in a tunnel four foot wide and just over five foot high, which caused them all to duck down slightly. Every few feet there was a crude wooden archway, built no doubt to give the tunnel stability and prevent cave-ins.

"Not much headroom," observed Firefly.

"I guess they just made the tunnel big enough so they could work in it comfortably;" suggested Miss Owl, "also less dirt for them to move and then store."

"C'mon," said The Wasp, "we'll take a quick look as to what's down here then we better get out of here; we're testing our luck as it is." And so, with The Wasp at the front, the three of them headed down through the tunnel where, after a short while, they came upon an empty alcove set into the wall which was six foot long and two foot high and seemed to be held in place by a wooden frame.

"Is that what I think it is?" asked Firefly warily.

"Yes, has to be," confirmed The Wasp nodding, "it's a coffin. Looks like when they find one they open up the side of it and then take out the remains."

"This whole thing is really starting to give me the creeps," said Miss Owl.

"I know," agreed The Wasp, "but we'll just look a little further. I want to see how far these tunnels go."

They continued onwards, working their way left and right through the maze of tunnels finding more and more empty alcoves as they went, until they found one where the skeleton was still in its resting place.

"This one's incomplete," said Firefly, noting that the lower jaw and most of the rib cage was missing. "I wonder if that's why they left it."

"Could well be," replied The Wasp. "Look, I think we've seen more than enough. It's time to leave."

The three then started to try to work their way back through the tunnels, but it soon became clear that something was wrong and they had become lost.

"Look, hold on," said The Wasp, stopping, "I think if we go back and …"

Suddenly the ground below them gave way and the three tumbled downwards.

Firefly landed on top of a large rectangular stone sarcophagus while The Wasp and Miss Owl landed on the earth floor with a bump.

"Everyone okay?" asked The Wasp, as he climbed to his feet.

"I think so," replied Firefly, as he got off the sarcophagus and looked at it, noting that a large chunk of the lid had broken off and was on the floor, "but I think that I've smashed this old coffin."

"No, I don't think you have," observed Miss Owl, as she stood up. "Looking at the state of it I think that it has been that way for some time."

The three looked around to fully take in their surroundings, to see that they were in a small stone chamber that was approximately twelve foot square; with the hole down which they had fallen about eighteen foot above them.

CHAPTER 5

"So we are in the church's vault?" asked Firefly. "Are there more of these chambers?"

"I'm not totally sure," said The Wasp, "we are down quite a way, much further than a six foot standard burial. I don't think that this was part of the church, it's more likely that this place was made first and then the church was built over it."

"So it was hidden deliberately?" suggested Miss Owl.

"I think so," replied The Wasp.

"Let's take a look inside the coffin," suggested Firefly, eyeing up the large open corner.

"No we can't do that!" cried Miss Owl in horror, "it's someone's grave."

"An ancient grave," pointed out Firefly quickly. "It's not as though there's going to be an actual body in there, just a pile of bones."

"Yes, but still," replied Miss Owl, unsure.

"I'm going to take a look," announced Firefly, as he moved to the broken end of the sarcophagus, with The Wasp following and they peered inside.

"Well?" asked Miss Owl.

"There is a body in there alright," confirmed Firefly excitedly. "I can see two skeletal feet wearing some sort of leather type sandal. I think whoever it is, is female. I can see a long dress." He paused, then moved round to the top of the coffin and looked over to The Wasp. "Take the other end; we can take the lid off to take a proper look."

"Oh no!" cried Miss Owl, "that's going too far!"

But it was too late.

Between them The Wasp and Firefly had lifted the broken stone lid and had carefully placed it down on the floor before going back to the coffin. With the deed done there was nothing Miss Owl could do but join them and see what was within.

Inside were indeed the remains of a woman, who would have been about five and a half foot tall, wearing a long red patterned dress with, as Firefly had said, brown sandals. Her skeletal hands were carefully arranged across her chest, holding a reddish pottery beaker. The skull had a full set of teeth and also a full head of long red hair which went down past the shoulders.

"Look at the dress," suggested Firefly, "it must be hundreds of years old, but looks brand new."

"And the bones themselves," added The Wasp, "they look so white I would have thought they would be yellowing after all this time."

"Come on," said Miss Owl uncomfortably, "you shouldn't have done that. Let her rest in peace."

The Wasp nodded. "Yes, you're right. Come on Firefly, let's put the lid back on and then we can worry about how we are going to get out of here."

"Hey! Hold on!" cried Miss Owl suddenly, "look, the cup she's holding, there's something funny about it."

The Wasp and Firefly looked down into the coffin to see that the pottery cup was starting to glow, with the light slowly growing getting brighter and filling the sarcophagus.

The Guardians found themselves standing back and shielding their eyes.

Then, the light suddenly faded into nothing. Cautiously, the three of them moved in again and looked down inside the coffin to see that the skeletal remains were gone. In their place, wearing the dress, was a young woman in her early twenties, with her eyes closed and her chest gently rising and falling as she breathed. Her eyelids suddenly flickered opened to reveal two blue eyes then, still holding the cup, she slowly stood up and first looked around the chamber and then in turn cast her eyes over Miss Owl, The Wasp and Firefly.

"Are, are you real?" asked Miss Owl eventually. "Or am I dreaming?"

"Yes, yes I am real," replied the woman; she spoke perfect English but without any trace of an accent.

"But how?" asked Firefly, looking towards the open sarcophagus. "A few moments ago you were just a pile of bones."

"I can only assume there is danger near and so I have been revived," she replied, "although I feel that this danger is not from yourselves; all I sense from you is overwhelming good."

The Guardians shuffled awkwardly.

"Where am I," asked the woman, "and what year is it?"

"Um, you are in a secret burial chamber under a church called St Mary's," answered The Wasp, "and as for the year it is 2019. Saturday 4th May to be exact."

The woman nodded, calmly taking in the information. "Then that means I have been buried for over a thousand years," she mused, before looking over at the Guardians again. "Who are you? And does everyone in this time dress in the strange way you do?"

"My name is Lucy, Lucy Randell," said Lucy, dispensing with the superhero alias, "and these are my two friends Glenn Keats and Will Hines."

The two young men nodded in acknowledgement.

"As for why we are dressed the way we are," Lucy continued, "that might take a little while to explain. Um, can I just ask, who are you exactly?"

"I am known as The Damsel of the Sanct Grael," she replied.

"Sanct Grael?" repeated Glenn, the wheels in his mind turning. "I've heard that before." Then his eyes widened in surprise. "Grael, as in Holy Grail?" His eyes went down to the cup that she held in her hands. "That's the Holy Grail! You are the keeper of the Holy Grail, the cup Jesus used at the last supper! The legends were true! It said that the Grail was brought to England and it's been hidden here all this time!"

The Damsel smiled and nodded. "Yes, I am the keeper of the Holy Grail. My family was entrusted with it to keep it hidden away from those who would use it and its power for their own ends, but it is not the Grail of the last supper. There is another, this one," she lifted it up to show them properly; "the *Emmaus Grail*."

"I've never heard of that," said Firefly, racking his brain.

"Let me explain;" said The Damsel, "after the crucifixion of Christ, two disciples were walking on the road to the village of Emmaus when they encountered a stranger who joined them. The stranger was puzzled as to why they were so sad, and they explained that Jesus had been killed, and that his body was now missing from the tomb. When they arrived at Emmaus the stranger went to head onwards, but the two disciples persuaded him to stay with them. They went to an inn and sat down for a meal. During this meal the stranger took the bread, blessed it and broke it. The two men then recognised the stranger as Jesus." The Damsel paused and lifted up the little stoneware cup. "At that meal there was also a cup, a cup which Jesus used and this is it. The Emmaus grail, the cup used by the living Christ."

The Guardians stared at the cup in awe.

"So how did it and you end up being buried here?" asked Will.

"I travelled to this land escaping a group of marauders who had found out about the grail and wanted it for their own," replied the Damsel. "While here I ended up under the protection of the Monks from Holme Abbey who agreed to protect me and the grail, and where I lived out my natural life."

"And after you died they buried you and the grail here," concluded Will.

"So it would seem," agreed the Damsel, nodding.

"Okay," said Lucy, "but what …"

"Hold on," broke in Glenn, "I think the time for questions is later: remember we still have to worry about the body snatchers finding us."

"Correction!" said a voice from above, "those 'body snatchers' as you so put it are already here!"

Everyone turned to look up to see two men looking down at them, dressed in overalls, that had just at that moment arrived on the scene. One had dark hair and a goatee and was in his forties, while the other was fair haired and clean shaven in his twenties.

CHAPTER 6

"Looks like we've been discovered Ron," said the man with the blonde hair.

"Nice one *Ben*!" replied Ron, as he cuffed his companion round the ear. "Why don't you give them our address and pin number as well?"

"Aw, sorry," he replied, as he rubbed his head.

"I told you about making sure that door was 'closed' properly, didn't I?" continued Ron angrily.

"Hey, I wasn't the last one out - I think," replied Ben sheepishly. He then looked down into the hole. "So, what do we do with them? We can't leave them there."

"And we can't let them escape either," replied Ron.

"You're not thinking of killing them are you?" asked Ben in alarm.

"I'm not sure what I'm thinking," said Ron, clearly flustered. "How many bodies are there left to dig out?"

"About eight that we can get to easily," answered Ben, "fifteen more difficult ones."

"So, how long would it take to get all twenty three, quickest scenario?" asked Ron.

"If I called for help," said Ben, "about a week."

Ron, looking annoyed, paused and gave a sigh and nodded. "Then that's what we'll have to do, not ideal I grant you. We'll do a dig and smash job then disappear as soon as."

"What about them?" asked Ben, looking down again into the chamber.

"We'll cover the hole over with planks and timbers then stack up the bags of dirt on top," suggested Ron, "that should keep them secure and out of our way. Once we've got the rest of the bodies and are off, we'll make an anonymous call to the police so they can come and find them."

"But that will give away our operation and they'll know our names," pointed out Ben.

"By then we'll be long gone," answered Ron, "and they haven't caught us yet!"

"But won't four missing youths attract a lot of attention in the meantime?" replied Ben. "Especially these lot; they're well known locally," he paused, "well apart from girly with the red hair. I've never seen her before."

"Can't be helped, I'm afraid," replied Ron. "We've got to make the best of a bad job."

"Hey, you can't do this!" cried Miss Owl.

"Can and will Miss," stated Ron dismissively, before turning back to Ben. "Right I'll stay here and keep an eye on them, you go back and get the boards."

"Shall I bring them some of our water bottles and food too?" asked Ben helpfully.

"Yeah, alright that's a good idea," replied Ron, "we can go to the store and replace them tomorrow."

Ben nodded and then disappeared from view.

Ron looked back down into the hole. "Don't worry you'll only be down here a few days. It won't be comfortable I grant you, but you'll survive."

"Sorry, but I have no intention of letting you bury us alive," insisted The Wasp defiantly, stepping forward and holding up his mobile phone smiling.

"Oh no!" cried Ron mockingly, as he put his hands to his cheeks. "He has a mobile phone, I bet they all do. All they have to do is call the police and they'll be rescued!" He moved his hands away from his face and glared. "Go on then." The challenge was issued in a slow deliberate tone.

Undeterred, The Wasp calmly went to his phone to dial 999, aiming to ask for the police, but quickly found that he couldn't. "Um, er, there's no signal," he said, "nothing. I can't get anything."

Immediately Miss Owl and Firefly went to their phones to try and, like The Wasp before them, found they couldn't get anything either.

"It's a strange phenomenon we discovered just after we started our excavations," said Ron, with a hint of triumph in his voice, "there's no signal down here at all. I'm no expert, but I think it might have something to do with the clay that's in the soil. Anyway, whatever the issue is your phones won't work, so there'll be no calling for help."

"Oh no!" cried Miss Owl. "So we are going to be stuck down here, buried alive till who knows when!"

"Not if I can help it," cried Firefly, who quickly jumped up on top of the stone casket and used it as a stepping stone to launch himself upwards towards the edge of the hole. Sadly though his efforts came up short and he missed the edge by about a foot and came crashing down again, landing in a heap on the floor where, helped by the others, he picked himself up.

"Pathetic!" retorted Ron. "Do you really think I'd let you just climb out. Lucky you missed." He then punched his hand three times; indicating what would have happened if he had managed to reach the edge. "Now be good little superheroes and stay where you are."

"No," said the Damsel, "I don't think we will. It is time for us to leave this place." And with that she lifted up the cup and, under her breath in ancient Aramaic, she started to speak.

"Hey, what you doing there?" snapped Ron.

The Wasp, Miss Owl and Firefly looked on in surprise as they had no idea what was happening either.

"I said 'what are you doing?'" repeated Ron loudly.

She ignored his question and continued. As she did so the beaker slowly started to glow. She abruptly stopped speaking and the vessel returned to its normal colour. She then looked up at him, the expression on her face changing. "Beware those that challenge me and the power I weald!"

"What?" demanded Ron warily, "are you some kind of witch or …"

He didn't get to finish the sentence.

A strange cream blur hit the man and knocked him off his feet and out of view. Then a few moments later there were screams of terror followed by silence.

"What did you do?" cried The Wasp. "You didn't kill him did you?"

"No, I merely summoned some help," replied the Damsel, sweetly. "He is no doubt unconscious, but alive."

"Help?" asked Lucy. "What kind of help?"

"You'll soon see," replied the Damsel. Just as she finished speaking the 'help' arrived.

Coming into view from above was a jaw-less and rib-less skeleton which knelt down by the hole.

"Oh my goodness the skeleton's alive!" cried Miss Owl.

"And it's the one that we saw earlier!" said Firefly, remembering the alcove in which they had seen the incomplete set of bones.

"You are acquainted with it?" asked the Damsel in surprise.

"Sort of," replied The Wasp, "we saw him as we went through the passages, but how?"

"I called forth the power of the cup for help," replied the Damsel, "and he answered."

"You brought an ancient skeleton to life!" said Firefly.

The Damsel nodded. "Not me, the cup, after all it is the cup of life."

By now the skeleton had lent forward and had extended his arm downwards and beckoned to them.

"Come, it is time for us all to go. I can no longer stay here and you do not belong here," the Damsel said with a smile. "Just climb on my sarcophagus, jump up and grab onto the skeleton's hand, he'll pull you up."

And so, taking a deep breath, Firefly jumped up, his hand outstretched, and was grabbed firmly by the skeleton that proceeded to pull him up and out of the tomb. The two then reached down and together pulled Miss Owl up and then The Wasp and finally the Damsel herself.

In the tunnel, crouching down due to the lack of height, the Guardians went to check on Ron, who was indeed unconscious.

"There's quite a large lump on his head," observed The Wasp, "but apart from that he'll be fine."

"Hey listen," cried Miss Owl suddenly, "I hear footsteps coming this way."

CHAPTER 7

"It's that Ben chap coming back with the boards," said The Wasp.

"Don't worry," replied the Damsel, "our new friend here will take care of him." She turned to the skeleton to direct him. "Go apprehend and restrain him." And instantly the skeleton disappeared off into the tunnel. A few moments later there was a cry followed by the sounds of a scuffle and a yell which, to the alarm of the Guardians, they instantly recognised.

"That's Carl!" cried Miss Owl.

The Guardians and the Damsel quickly made their way towards the yelling to find Carl, in his Blue Bolt costume, with the jawless skeleton sitting on his chest pinning him down.

"No, call him off," cried The Wasp in alarm. "That's our friend Carl, Blue Bolt, he's one of us."

The Damsel nodded and instantly the skeleton released Blue Bolt who, fighting for breath, yelled, "That's a zombie skeleton! It tried to get me."

"It's alright," said Miss Owl, who went to him and helped him to his feet, "he's with us."

"But how? And who are you?" he asked, noticing the stranger in the red patterned dress.

"I am The Damsel of Sanct Grael," replied the woman.

"Danielle?" said Blue Bolt, mishearing her title.

"Er, Yes, well, why not?" said Firefly. "We can't keep calling her 'the Damsel' all of the time can we?"

"Or better still, how about Danni?" suggested Miss Owl.

Danni smiled and nodded, happy with this new name.

"So?" pressed Blue Bolt. "Who exactly is she and what's going on?" He glanced over to the skeleton with some apprehension.

"Hold on, first things first," said The Wasp. "If you're here you must have seen the body snatching operation. Did you encounter a young blonde chap called Ben?"

"Oh, was that his name?" asked Blue Bolt with a smile. "Yes I saw him. Lively chap; thought he would try to attack me with a spade. It didn't go well for him of course; he's nicely tied up now."

"Good work," said The Wasp with some relief, knowing they didn't have to worry about him anymore, "but how did you know to come here in the first place? You were supposed to be taking it easy at home."

"I was," replied Blue Bolt, "I was following you all on the tracer app on my phone. I saw you go into the church and then suddenly your signals disappeared. I thought you might be in trouble so I got changed into my costume and came along to help."

"That chap Ron did say that there was no phone signal down here," said Miss Owl. "The app must have failed when we entered the tunnels."

"Ron? Who's Ron?" asked Blue Bolt.

"Alright we better fill you in on what we've been up to and who exactly Danni is," said The Wasp, who then went on to tell him about their adventure.

"Wow!" said Blue Bolt when he had finished, looking Danni up and down. "That is incredible! The police are going to have a field day with this."

"Police?" asked Danni. "What is Police?"

"They enforce the law," explained Firefly.

"No, I cannot see them," replied Danni, shaking her head. "I and the grail must stay a secret. If word were to get out I have no idea what will happen."

"That's true enough," said Miss Owl, "I'm sure there will be all kinds of people wanting it, especially considering the power it has."

"Er, um, yeah," stumbled Blue Bolt awkwardly, "about that. I'm afraid we have a problem."

"What do you mean?" asked Firefly.

"When I got to the cottages here and realised that something was really wrong I called them," explained Blue Bolt, "they should be here soon."

"We've got to hide her," Miss Owl urged instantly.

"Agreed," said The Wasp, "Lucy do you think you can manage to get her out of here and keep her safe?"

"Yes, of course," she replied, "my parents are away for the Bank Holiday so she can stay with me."

"Good," replied The Wasp, "we can meet you there tomorrow. In the meantime myself, Will and Carl can deal with the police. We'll of course cover for you so they will have no idea you were here or the existence of Danni."

"But what about Ben and Ron?" prompted Firefly. "They've both seen Lucy and Danni."

"Blast, that's right," said The Wasp. "I'd forgotten about them, that's thrown a spanner in the works."

"Perhaps I can help with that," said Danni, holding the grail up, "one touch and I can erase the memory of them seeing us."

"Alright," said The Wasp, "that seems our only option."

"But what about our skeletal friend here?" asked Blue Bolt, looking at the resurrected skeleton which seemed to be waiting patiently for its next order.

"That won't be an issue," assured Danni, who turned to it, smiled and nodded. "Thank you for your help, you may return to the place from which you came."

In response the skeleton gave a little bow and then turned and disappeared back down the tunnel to return to its coffin. The small group quickly returned to where Ron was still lying unconscious. Danni gently placed the grail on his forehead and again whispered in ancient Aramaic. The cup glowed briefly and she confirmed that when he awoke he would have no memory of her or Lucy. They made their way back to the cottages where Danni dealt with Ben in the same way, wiping his memory. Just as she finished they heard the sound of sirens. Taking their cue Lucy and Danni secretly left the cottages by one of the back doors.

As this was happening Glenn, Will and Carl, knowing they would have to give a statement to the police, quickly went over the story they would give making sure they left out the details about Danni and Lucy being with them. The other embellishment they made was that it was Carl who tackled Ron and helped the others out of the hidden 'empty' chamber. They then went to meet the two police officers, who they encountered as they entered the graveyard via the main gate. Carl, who had made the call, then went to explain what he had found. They took the officers to the back of the buildings and into the cottages where they saw it for themselves. On realising what they were facing, the Officers first put a call in to the station for immediate back up and while they waited for it to arrive they called an ambulance for Ron and Ben who, both now awake, were formally placed under arrest. Then the officers, using the police tape fetched from their patrol car, created a perimeter around the church to seal off what would be declared a major crime scene. A short while later Sargent Singh, along with two plain clothed detectives, arrived on the scene and officially took over. It was at this point that Glenn, Will and Carl received a group text from Lucy saying that she and Danni had safely made it to her house.

Sargent Singh took immediate charge of The Guardians; first telling them off for going into the graveyard and putting themselves in danger, but then congratulating them on uncovering such a major criminal activity. He then arranged for them to be taken to the police station, via the comic shop to pick up their 'civilian clothes' where, as they rehearsed, they gave their statements. After this was done, the three of them were instructed to keep off social media about the night's events and not to speak to the press in any form. Once this was done, which was just after midnight, the

Custody Sargent arranged for a car and the three were taken to their individual homes.

CHAPTER 8

Glenn, Will and Carl, dressed in their everyday casual clothes, arrived at Lucy's house at 10.00 am.

They were greeted by Lucy herself who led them through to the lounge where Danni, now wearing Lucy's old koala bear onesie, was seated on a large sofa staring up at the plasma TV, which was on the wall above the fireplace, watching a cartoon. In front of her, on the large coffee table, was an open laptop and next to that a tablet and Lucy's mobile phone, all of which she seemed to be using at the same time. Also on the table was a large cup of coffee, a plate of pastries and a jug of orange juice. Next to that, resting on a coaster, was the Emmaus Grail itself.

"And welcome to the 21st Century!" exclaimed Glenn, with a smile. "You seem to be settling in quite well with all the basics covered. With that onesie we'll have to start calling you 'Koala Girl'!"

Danni looked over to him, with a look of awe etched on her face as she motioned around her. "Such wonders! The world that you live in is so advanced." She picked up the tablet. "Magical devices that bring moving pictures, electronic music and the knowledge of the world; as well as games with exploding fruit and sheep."

"She's basically been up all night catching up on things," explained Lucy, sitting down beside her. "I showed her how the TV and internet worked and just left her to it."

"And she seems to have mastered things well enough," noted Carl with a smile as he, along with Will and Glenn, sat down on the second sofa.

"She's a very quick learner," stated Lucy. "Hey, have you seen today's news?"

Glenn and Will had but Carl, who got up later, hadn't so Lucy took the tablet and, on the big TV, called up the news report that she had seen earlier. It showed pictures of St Mary's church, now totally sealed off, with a flurry of activity by police officers and forensic teams. Also in the background were images of a number of other news teams who had heard about the breaking story. The news report outlined that a major body snatching venture had been discovered and that dozens of skeletons had been stolen over, what was believed to be, a nine month period. It went on to say that two arrests had already been made and others were expected to follow.

"Oh wow," enthused Carl, "looks like we stumbled upon a massive nationwide operation. There's no mention of us though."

"Not at the moment," corrected Glenn, "but I'm sure there will soon; and there's bound to be a big court case at some point down the line where we have to give evidence."

"Looks like we did the right thing keeping Danni out of things," remarked Will.

"Although my existence is known about," she said, with a hint of pride, "well, in a manner of speaking anyway." She then reached and took the tablet back from Lucy and tapped the screen. On the TV appeared a portrait of a red haired woman holding an elaborate goblet, above her was a white dove and underneath the picture was the caption 'The Damsel of Sanct Grael by Dante Gabriel Rossetti - 1874'.

"Wow!" exclaimed Will in surprise. "That is *you*, but the grail is totally wrong; it's a metal goblet, not a pottery beaker."

"I know," said Lucy excitedly, "that grail is supposed to be the one from the Last Supper. Now here's the thing, there is no reference *anywhere* about the Emmaus Grail. We tried to look it up and found nothing, not a trace of it in books, fact or fiction, film, TV, historical journals, or even religious art. It's not even mentioned in the 'The Road to Emmaus' bible passage itself. As far as the modern world is concerned the Emmaus Grail has never existed."

"Which is good in one respect," observed Will. "If no-one knows about it then it stands to reason that no-one will be looking for it, so Danni and the grail are safe; for the moment anyway."

"What do you mean by that?" asked Carl.

"What happens when people do find out about her and the grail?" asked Glenn.

"Well I'm not going to say anything about her," replied Lucy hotly.

This was followed by a murmur of agreement from Will and Carl.

"Of course you're not," said Glenn quickly, "and neither am I, but things have a habit of coming out no matter what you say or do."

"I don't see how," retorted Will, slightly confused.

"Okay," explained Glenn, "look at Danni herself. She has just literally appeared into existence yesterday. No birth certificate, hospital or doctor's records, no work or educational history and certainly no exams or qualifications. How is that going to be explained? People are going to ask questions as to how and why she has no personal history and I'm not sure I can come up with a plausible answer for that, can you?"

The others looked at each other hoping that someone would come up with a suitable answer, but no-one did.

"And then there is the issue of the grail itself," he continued. "What happens to it? Can you imagine if someone with sinister intentions gets hold of it?"

"We could rebury it somewhere or put it in a bank vault," suggested Lucy. "That should keep it safe."

"No," said Danni firmly, "I cannot be separated from the grail, even for a moment. The task has been given to me alone and I must honour it."

"Well, you wandering around with a pottery cup all the time is certainly going to raise eyebrows and questions," admitted Carl.

"Hey, what about the monks that originally protected Danni and the grail?" exclaimed Will suddenly. "Could they help again?"

"Yes, of course," said Danni, "The Brothers of Holme, they would certainly protect me and the grail as they did before."

"That's assuming they still exist," pointed out Carl. "A thousand years is a long time."

Lucy took back the tablet from Danni, made a quick internet search, and called up on the TV screen the address.

"Looks like we're in business," said Glenn, with a smile, "not only is it still active, but it's about an hour and a half away."

"They don't seem to have a telephone number or e-mail," noted Carl, looking at the screen.

"They must be one of those orders that shun modern life," suggested Will.

"So what are they doing in a directory?" asked Carl.

"I'm guessing it's the type where they just find organisations details and publish without asking," replied Lucy, "which is fortunate as otherwise we might not have had a way to find them."

"Well luckily we have," said Glenn, "and if we can't call or e-mail them then that leaves us with one option; to visit them in person. I think that there is no time like the present."

"Now, this second?" asked Lucy in surprise. "I was going to take her into town this afternoon and show her around."

"The sooner we can get her and the grail to safety the better," said Glenn.

A look of clear disappointment crossed Lucy's face.

"I'm afraid that he's right," conceded Danni reluctantly, "and as much as I would like to see your world first hand, there is a real danger, that in doing so, I might decide that I would like to become part of it. No, we must go now."

Lucy nodded, realising that it was for the best.

"Alright," said Glenn, "we can all go in my car."

Danni stood up and picked up the grail. "Right, let's go."

Lucy started to giggle. "Alright," she said, "but perhaps first, I think you had better change."

Danni looked at herself and started to blush. She had totally forgotten that she was still wearing Lucy's koala bear onesie.

CHAPTER 9

It was just before two o'clock in the afternoon that they arrived at Holme Friary. The five of them found themselves standing in front of a large sprawling Victorian house on the green. They would have got there sooner but, as lunch was approaching, they decided to stop off and eat at a roadside café and then, despite the Sat Nav, they had problems finding the little road which led onto the secluded, almost hidden, estate.

"Wow!" exclaimed Carl, as he looked the building over. "This house looks creepy, something straight out of a horror movie."

"Are you sure this is the place?" asked Danni. "This is certainly not the Friary I remember."

"It's the address from the directory," confirmed Lucy. "I'm afraid the other one may not exist anymore, a lot of them were destroyed. I would guess that the order carried on in a more modest setting."

"Come on," said Glenn, "let's see if there is anyone at home." And with that he walked up to the large oak door and banged on it.

After a few moments there was the sound of footsteps and the door slowly opened to reveal one of the monks. The man was in his early forties and had black hair cut short with a fringe. He was dressed in a mustard coloured robe made from wool, tied at the waist with a long white cord. On his left arm there was a black cloth band and on his feet he wore brown sandals. "Yes?" he asked, looking at the small group with some surprise. "Can I help?"

"Um, yes," said Glenn nervously, "we would like to see the Abbot please. We have something of the utmost importance to speak to him about."

A sad look crossed the Monk's face. "I am afraid that will not be possible."

"Look I know it might be inconvenient,

especially on a Sunday," pressed Lucy, "but this is really important."

"No, you don't understand," replied the Monk, as he motioned to his armband. "The Abbot is no longer with us. He passed away last night."

The Guardians gave a collective gasp.

"Oh, I am so sorry," said Glenn quickly, "I didn't realise that's what you meant but, please, what we have to say is really urgent. Is there anyone else that we can see? There must be an acting Abbot, second in command, or someone else."

"No, I'm very sorry," replied the Monk, shaking his head, "we are a reclusive order. We do not accept visitors at normal times, let alone in a time of mourning."

"Please," begged Danni, stepping forward holding the grail in both hands, "he'll want to see me."

The Monk's eyes fell on the cup and looked at Danni with puzzlement.

"I am The Damsel of the Sanct Grael," she continued, "the keeper of the grail used by Christ at the village of Emmaus. Over a thousand years ago I called upon the monks of this order for help to protect me and I have need to do so again."

The Monk's eyes widened in surprise; which was then quickly replaced by a higher understanding and belief. "Um, alright, I think you had all better come in," he said, in a shaky voice.

He stood back, opening the door wider allowing the small group to enter into the large hallway dominated by a sweeping staircase. "Please wait here," asked the Monk, as he closed the door. "I will fetch Brother Gilbert, the Dean." He then disappeared off leaving the group to wait.

After a few minutes there came the sound of hurried footsteps and the Monk, who let them into the building, appeared with an elderly man with neatly combed white hair and black rimmed glasses. "I am the Dean, Brother Gilbert," said the newcomer, looking straight at Danni. "Brother Mortimer here says that you claim to be the bearer of the Holy Grail."

She nodded and held up the cup.

The Dean stared at it in surprise and awe. "How on earth is this possible?"

The Damsel then proceeded to tell him the tale

of how her family had kept the grail hidden and that the Monks of the Friary protected her. Lucy then took over the story and explained about the body snatchers, Danni's resurrection and that they decided to bring her here for safety, while the Dean listened intently. "Ah yes," he said at the end, "we saw the news report last night about St Mary's." He glanced at Lucy, Glenn, Will and Carl. "So you are the famous costumed superheroes?"

Glenn and the others nodded.

"Well," continued the Dean, looking back at Danni, "if it is sanctuary that you seek, then we shall be more than happy to help. It will be an honour to continue with the task that our ancient brethren started. We shall find you suitable quarters. Please regard the Friary as your new home, where we will be at your disposal."

"Thank you," replied Danni, who was visibly relieved that she and the grail would again be safe.

The Dean looked down hesitantly at the cup. "You say that that cup gave 'life' to skeletons hundreds of years old?"

She nodded. "Yes."

"Would it work on a more recently deceased person?" he continued coyly.

Brother Mortimer gave a gasp. "Surely you are not thinking of …" he left the words hanging, not daring to finish the sentence.

"Why not?" replied the Dean. He glanced over to Danni. "Is it possible? Could the grail revive the Abbot? He is a good man with strong and wise leadership and we need his council. The truth is the order would be lost without him."

"Yes, it is possible," agreed Danni, smiling, "and I will be more than happy to do so. Using the power of the grail, there will be no problem in bringing him back."

"And will he be completely restored as he was before?" asked the Dean.

"Yes, he will," confirmed Danni, "it will be as though he will wake from a long sleep; which of course in a sense is what will happen. I will be happy to help you. Where is he?"

"After Brother Campbell, who used to be a Doctor in his former life, pronounced him dead; siting a heart attack as the cause," explained Brother Mortimer, "the Abbot was laid out in his room. He's there now while the chapel was being prepared for him."

"Then please lead us there," instructed Danni.

Immediately, the two monks headed towards the main staircase. Danni and the Guardians followed. At the top of the stairs they took a right down a small corridor, eventually arriving at a door marked 'Abbot'. Taking a key from his robe, the Dean opened the door and the small group entered, finding themselves in a large room that seemed to be a cross between a sitting room and a study, with a large desk and a free standing floor safe by it. Positioned around a large fire, that had a large plasma TV over the mantle, was a green leather Winchester style sofa and chairs. One wall was dominated by a large bookcase that was filled with both books and DVD's, while the other was covered with artwork.

"He's through here in the bedroom," said the Dean, pointing to a closed wood panelled door. Continuing to lead the way he crossed through the room and then opened the door and entered. The small group followed and there, on a large oak bed, was the body of the Abbot; the blankets pulled up to his chest, but with his arms outside them, straight by his sides. Covering each eyelid was a large gold coin and on his face were traces of a slight smile.

"Behold," said the Dean sadly, "Abbot Morley."

CHAPTER 10

With everyone watching with bated breath, Danni moved forward to the Abbot. Noticing a small jug of water on the bedside table she picked it up and poured some into the grail and then placed the jug back down. Over the forehead of the Abbot she tipped the grail, allowing a few drops of water to spill out, as she spoke in ancient Aramaic. Almost at once the Abbot's ashen complexion started to change as colour rushed back to his face. She then moved the cup to the Abbot's lips and again tipping it, allowed the rest of the water to drip into his mouth before standing back. After a few moments, the Abbot slowly took in a deep breath and his chest began to rise and fall rhythmically. Very slowly he sat himself up in the bed, the two coins on his eyes falling away as he did so, landing on the floor with a clatter.

"Abbot, are you, are you alright?" asked the Dean tentatively, as he moved closer to the bed.

Slowly the Abbot nodded. "Yes, yes I am," he replied, "I must confess when I went to bed last night I felt terrible. I started to have slight chest pains. I was about to call for help, but I must have fallen asleep. Now I feel - I feel fantastic!" He turned to look at Danni and the rest of the Guardians who were looking on. "Who are you and what are you doing in my private chamber?" He then looked over to the Dean. "What exactly is going on here? Why are you wearing a black band on your arm? Who has died?"

"Abbot there is a lot to explain to you." He turned to Brother Mortimer. "Please could you be kind enough to take our guests down to the main sitting room and arrange some refreshments for them while I fill the Abbot in on what has been happening."

Brother Mortimer nodded and he led Danni and the Guardians out of the Abbot's bedroom through the sitting room / study and back out into the main house, taking them downstairs to a large communal sitting room where they seated themselves on sofas by an unlit fireplace. Brother Mortimer then rang a pull cord by the fireside. Shortly afterwards another monk appeared and he ordered him to fetch refreshments, explaining that the Abbot had been restored and would be joining them. The monk, somewhat surprised, nodded and disappeared off leaving the small group waiting for about fifteen minutes. When he returned he was pushing a small serving trolley on top of which was a large tea pot and a coffee pot as well as fine bone china cups and saucers, while on the second shelf plates of sandwiches and cakes. He then proceeded to serve everyone before eventually departing, taking the trolley with him. A short while after that the door to the Sitting room opened again and in came the Abbot, now dressed in his mustard robe, and the Dean who had now taken off the black mourning band. The two went straight over to the small group, where the Abbot's attention went straight to the grail sitting on the table and then to Danni. "Brother Gilbert has told me who you are and what happened. Thank you - thank you for saving my... no that's not quite right is it? Thank you for *giving* me my life back."

Danni smiled. "That is quite alright, I am glad to be of help. How are you feeling?"

The Abbot paused. "Fit and well, better than I have been in over twenty years." From his pocket he produced a pair of spectacles and shrugged. "Even these are not required any more, my vision is now perfect." He dropped them onto the table. "Brother Gilbert has told me that he has sanctioned your request for sanctuary. This decision, in my 'absence,' will of course be honoured."

"Thank you," replied Danni gratefully, "it is vitally important that the grail is kept a secret from the world. In the wrong hands the power it could weald could be devastating."

"Yes, absolutely," replied The Abbot, again glancing down at the grail, "rest assured your presence here, along with the grail, will become our number one priority. We shall protect you as our ancient Brothers did all that time ago." He paused. "In fact it will be an honour to hear from you the stories and accounts of what the Friary was like all those years ago and I am also very keen, if you are willing to teach me, to learn ancient Aramaic."

"Of course," replied Danni, with a smile, "it will be an honour to teach you and tell you about my life."

"And speaking of interesting tales," continued the Abbot, turning to the Guardians, "I am interested to hear about your exploits patrolling the streets dressed as superheroes. Please tell me everything."

"Well," began Glenn, "it all started about two

years ago through my love of comic books …"

For the next couple of hours the Guardians talked and chatted with the Abbot and Dean who, along with Danni, listened intently. However, it was as the large Grandfather clock in the corner struck 5 o'clock that the Abbot brought the meeting to a close. "Ah!" he said, standing glancing over at the clock. "As much as I would like to hear more of your adventures and get to know you all better, I am afraid that the evensong service draws near and of course I must oversee the preparations for the Damsel's stay, as well as addressing the Brothers about my return."

The Guardians and Danni stood up.

"That's alright," said Glenn, "we ought to be making a move ourselves."

"And from the bottom of our hearts," continued the Abbot, "thank you for bringing the Damsel and the Grail to us. I promise you they will be well looked after."

"That's alright," replied Lucy, "under the circumstances it seemed the only logical thing to do." She turned to Danni. "Hopefully we'll be able to visit you soon."

"Ah, alas, I am afraid that will not be possible," replied the Abbot sadly. "You were only permitted into the Friary because of the uniqueness of the situation that presented itself with The Damsel and the grail. We cannot allow visits."

"Oh," said Lucy, clearly disappointed.

"Also," continued the Dean, "you coming here could potentially risk exposing the existence of the Damsel and the Grail and could even result in yourself being in danger, if some threatening party wanted to use you to get to us"

"He's right you know," agreed Carl sadly.

"Now," said the Abbot, turning to Danni, "I understand from the Dean that the Grail has the power to erase memories. You did so with those two grave robbers."

She nodded. "Yes, it is able to do that."

"Well," continued the Abbot, "I think that under the circumstances you should use that ability on your friends here. As long as they know about you and the grail there is a danger that somehow it will be revealed."

Danni paused, looking uncomfortable about the idea, but then thinking about it she slowly nodded. "Yes, you are quite right, that does seem the best course of action to take under the circumstances." She then carefully picked up the Grail and turned to the Guardians. "Thank you so much for all your assistance. I have no idea what I would have done without you. After we have said our goodbyes and you leave here, all memory of me will slowly disappear over the next few hours. But rest assured, I will always remember you and the kindness you showed me." As she finished speaking, the Grail slowly started to glow.

CHAPTER 11

Thursday night had always been games night.

Glenn, Will and Carl would meet at Lucy's house about seven in the evening and they would spend two hours or so playing whatever board game they had agreed upon. Once they had finished, Glenn would take over and go over the details of the following two days patrol in the town centre, before they all headed off home.

Gathered round the dining room table, surrounded by drinks and snacks, tonight's game was called 'The Wizard of Castle Tremore', a medieval fantasy adventure which involved hunting down and defeating a renegade Wizard in his trap filled lair.

Will rolled the twenty-sided die and watched it land on a fifteen. This allowed him to cast a spell on his chosen opponent which, in this case, was the Wizard's young apprentice. From the cards he held in his hand he put one down on the board. "Silence spell," he said, "the apprentice will not be able to speak for the next round and therefore can't cast any spells."

"Hold on a second," said Carl, "I know you've got the 'Amnesia card' in your pack, you took it from me on your last go, why not use that instead, that will keep him out of things for the next three rounds?"

Will paused and shrugged. "Well, we are all aware that that kind of thing doesn't work aren't we?" He looked around the table at his friends, all of whom suddenly looked slightly uncomfortable. "Danni said we would forget her in a matter of hours and yet here days later and I remember everything."

"I know," replied Lucy, "we all do."

"Then what about the body snatchers?" he continued. "If we remember Danni and the grail, do you think they do too?"

"Highly unlikely," replied Glenn. "If they did, the Police would already be in contact with us by now."

"So why do we remember then?" pressed Will.

"Perhaps that was Danni's parting gift to us?" suggested Lucy.

"But it was decided that if we remember her and the grail it may put us all in danger," pointed out Carl. "I'm sure that she wouldn't want that."

Lucy shrugged. "I'm sorry, but I'm afraid that I just don't have an answer. Perhaps if we …"

THUD!

Everyone turned to the source of the sudden sound, the dining room window, to see a large white pigeon that had flown into the glass and was now perched on the window ledge flapping its wings and scratching at the plastic frame. However, this was not like an ordinary pigeon they had seen before - this particular pigeon had no head.

"That's gross,' exclaimed Carl, "I know chickens run around when their heads are cut off, but I had no idea the same kind of thing applied to pigeons."

"It doesn't," replied Lucy bluntly, "there's only one possible explanation for it."

"Danni," exclaimed Glenn, "she's the only person we know who has the capability of bringing a dead bird back to life."

"She must be in some kind of trouble and this is her way of asking for help," concluded Lucy.

"So much for the Abbot and the Monks protecting her," said Carl.

"Actually," suggested Lucy warily, "I think it might be more a case that she needs our help to protect her from the Abbot and the Monks,"

"You're right," agreed Glenn, "I bet that was why she didn't wipe our memories. She must have somehow had doubts about them and thought she might need to call us for help."

"Which she's done by sending that bird," chipped in Carl.

"After raising it back to life," concluded Will, "and if that's the way she decided to reach us, she must be in a real jam."

"Right then Guardians," said Glenn, standing, "we need to get ourselves suited up and go back to the Friary as soon as possible. 'Koala Girl' and the Grail are in trouble. We'll meet back here in an hour. I'll drive."

And then, as though somehow understanding that its message had been received and understood, the headless pigeon flapped its wings and flew away.

Two hours later, under the cover of night, The Guardians, in their full superhero costumes, arrived at the road that led into the Friary estate. The Wasp pulled his car over on the small verge and the group got out, having decided to make the remainder of the journey on foot. A short while later they arrived at the end of the small tree lined path which opened out to reveal the main grounds and house.

"So what now?" asked Firefly. "We can't just go up and knock on the front door and ask if they're holding Danni hostage."

Before anyone could answer, the headless pigeon reappeared. It flew over their heads and landed in front of them. The creature hopped and flapped its wings then took off again, landing a short distance away to their right where it again started to flap its wings, before making another short flight in the same direction.

"Um, I think it wants us to follow it," said Miss Owl, "I bet it will take us straight to Danni!"

"I guess it makes sense," said The Wasp, "after all, she's the one who sent it. C'mon, follow that pigeon!" And with that he slowly moved forwards with the rest of the Guardians following. Again, somehow understanding that its message had been understood, the pigeon carried on, with its short flights, leading the Guardians in a wide circle to the right of the building into the grounds of the Friary, seemingly aiming towards a large grass covered mound, in the entrance of which was a large six foot wrought iron gate that was heavily padlocked. In one last push, the pigeon flew straight towards the gate and landed just outside. From within a familiar redheaded figure appeared.

"Danni!" cried Miss Owl, as she and the rest of the Guardians arrived at the gate. "Are you alright? What happened?"

Danni smiled, visibly relieved to see her friends. "The Monks turned on me," she quickly explained. "For the first couple of days everything was fine. I spent time with the Abbot and the Dean, explaining to them about the grail and showing them the power it held, then one night they and the Monks attacked me. They took the grail and then bundled me into this place, which they called the Ice-house. Luckily, with the residual power I held from the cup, I was able to resurrect a dead pigeon and send it to you. Thank goodness that I decided at the last moment not to erase the memory you had of me! Can you get me out of here?"

"Easily!" said Blue Bolt confidently.

"Good, but hurry!" pressed Danni.

With a nod he stepped forward, taking from his utility belt a small leather case which he opened and produced a long tool with a hooked end. "In real life I'm a trainee Locksmith. I'll have you out in a jiffy," he explained to Danni, before going to the lock. After a few moments there was a click and he removed it. He then went to try to open the gate but it would not move.

"It's stuck solid," said Blue Bolt, "I don't think that it even needed to be bolted shut!"

"Here, let me," said Firefly, "I may not have 'super strength' but thanks to the hours I spend in the gym, I'm stronger than most."

Blue Bolt stood to one side. Firefly stepped forward and grabbed hold of the gate and pulled hard on it. First it stayed in place then, using all his strength on the second try, the door flew open. Just as it came free Danni stepped out of her makeshift prison cell and, as she did so, the headless pigeon flew up into the air and disappeared into the darkness.

CHAPTER 12

"Thank you," said Danni gratefully. "Now we must retrieve the Grail. The Abbot is keeping it in the safe in his study."

"Ah! I remember it," said Blue Bolt, "it's a Miller & Singer. The firm went out of business in the 1920's. I should be able to crack the combination on it, but it may take some time."

"First things first though," said The Wasp, "we need to get into the Friary."

"There are two doors that lead into the cellar at the back of the house," said Danni. "That will take us into the kitchen and we can get into the main house from there."

"Perfect," said The Wasp, "show us where it is."

And so leading the way, with the Guardians following, Danni headed towards the Friary, taking them round the building until they arrived at two large wooden doors set into the ground, which had a large padlock on them. Without a word Blue Bolt moved forward with his lock pick and, in a few moments, the padlock was opened and discarded. Then he, with the help of Firefly, opened the large door to reveal a small flight of stone steps. From their belts each of the Guardians took their torches and turned them on to light the way, then the group descended down the stairs into the basement, which they found was filled with wooden crates of all shapes and sizes as well as a number of old fashioned Tea Chests.

"I wonder what on earth is in all these," said Miss Owl, shining her torch around.

"One way to find out," stated Firefly, as he moved to one of the open crates and looked inside.

"Well?" asked Miss Owl.

Firefly reached into the crate and pulled out a brand new semi-automatic rifle. "There are about a dozen of them in here," he confirmed.

"Monks with weapons?" queried Miss Owl.

"Apparently so," replied Firefly.

"Right," said The Wasp, looking round, "let's see what else is here."

And so the Guardians started to examine the other wooden boxes that filled the cellar, where they found more guns as well as ammunition, grenades, vintage wines, art, silverware, and a variety of other antiques.

"What the heck have we stumbled upon?" asked Firefly.

"I'm not totally sure," replied The Wasp, "but whatever it means I think it points to the fact that it's even more crucial we get the grail and Danni out of here as fast as we can."

Leaving the crates behind, The Guardians moved across the large cellar to the other side where another flight of stairs took them up and through a door into the deserted kitchen. Carefully opening the door and checking there was no one about they made their way along a short corridor, finding themselves in the familiar surroundings of the main hall. Turning their torches off and putting them away they made their way up the main staircase and back down the short corridor to the Abbot's rooms where Blue Bolt placed his ear against the door and listened, before moving away. "I can't hear anything," he confirmed, "hopefully he's asleep." Then, trying the handle, he pushed at the door slightly and peeked inside, before looking back and nodding. "It's alright, there's no one about. I'm going to need light, but not too much."

In response The Wasp and Miss Owl took out their torches again and turned them on. Then Blue Bolt slowly opened the door and went inside with the rest of the group following. Firefly, who was the last, closed the door again carefully.

The small group made their way to the safe where Blue Bolt knelt down in front of it with Miss Owl and The Wasp shining their torches on him so he could see what he was doing. Blue Bolt placed his ear against the safe's door and with his left hand took hold of the dial and proceeded to turn it left, then right, then left again. He stayed working at the safe for almost fifteen minutes before kneeling back shaking his head. "It's no good," he said in despair, "the first of the tumblers dropped in place okay, but the others aren't, no matter what I try. I'm sorry, but I'm afraid that I just can't do it."

"Oh what a shame that is," said a familiar voice, as the main light of the room switched on.

Everyone turned towards the voice to see the Abbot dressed in his Mustard robe standing in the doorway that led to his private quarters. In his hand was a modern looking handgun which he pointed at the group. "I've been watching you from my room since you came in. I'm very impressed you thought you could break in and snatch the grail from under my nose, but I'm afraid it's time to bring a stop to your little venture. Now get up and move away from the safe."

Blue Bolt got to his feet and the group moved away as they were instructed.

"So," The Abbot said, addressing Danni directly as he moved into the room, "how did you manage to make contact with the rest of your friends and let them know you were in trouble?"

"Would you believe that I resurrected a dead pigeon and sent it for help?" she replied.

The Abbot nodded. "After the past few days with you I'm willing to accept a lot of things."

"Apart from the promise you made to protect her and the grail it seems," accused The Wasp.

"Ah, but I'm afraid that that was never really an option," replied The Abbot, with a sly smile. "You see, the harsh reality of things is that I and the Monks here have nothing to do with the original 'Holme Order'. They were disbanded in the year 1538 by King Henry VIII as part of his dissolution of the Monasteries when he broke away from the Catholic Church. In the 1850's the house we are in now was built on the original site which I bought about twenty years ago and established this 'Friary' and I use the word in the loosest possible sense. To the outside world we are a band of Monks who keep themselves to themselves and humbly pray to God. However, the truth is very different. I have set up a haven for those, like myself, who seek not to be bothered by the law. Each of the 'Monks' has their own dark criminal story; bank robbers, fraudsters, murderers, forgers, you find us all here."

"And what about the crates in the kitchen cellar?" asked Blue Bolt.

"Ah, so you've been busy exploring have you?" said the Abbot. "Well, we also do a spot of gun running on the side as well as making stolen and illegal items available on the black market to the highest bidder."

"And is that what you had in mind for the grail?" asked The Wasp.

"Oh no," replied the Abbot, shaking his head, "I had much bigger plans for that. A cup with that power was going to elevate us to a whole new level. There are people who will pay literally half of their fortunes in order to cheat death or be healed from illness or disability."

"You cannot use the cup of Christ in this way," protested Danni.

"Oh, we can and we will," replied the Abbot, with an evil smile. "And I'm afraid that there is nothing you can do to stop it."

"Blast it!" said Blue Bolt. "If only I had been quicker and better equipped. I could have had that safe open and we could have been clean away by now."

"Oh you fool, you have no idea how close you came to succeeding," said the Abbot, with a smile.

He then moved over to the safe. "You see the truth is, the tumblers in this thing are broken and have never worked. The safe was *already* unlocked."

And to demonstrate this, the Abbot turned the handle and the door of the safe slowly creaked open.

CHAPTER 13

The Guardians looked at each other in shock and surprise.

The Abbot smiled and shook his head. "What a sorry bunch you are, pretending to be heroes and dressed up in silly costumes."

"Says the man wearing a mustard bathrobe impersonating a Monk," retorted Miss Owl swiftly.

"And we *are* heroes," pressed Blue Bolt, "we do a lot of good and help a lot of people."

"You don't look very heroic now," replied the Abbot scornfully. "You look like a scared bunch of kids out of your depth, mind you hardly surprising as I'm holding a gun."

"Then put it down and make it an easy fight," challenged Firefly defiantly.

"Not a chance!" replied the Abbot as, keeping the gun trained on them, he moved back towards the desk, picked up the phone, pressed a button on the key pad and put the receiver to his ear. After a few moments whoever he called responded and a muffled voice could be heard.

"It's me," replied the Abbot, "we've had a problem; those meddling Guardians turned up and freed the Damsel. They then tried to steal the Grail from the safe."

From the phone there came an expletive.

"Don't worry," replied the Abbot, "I managed to stop them. I have them here in my rooms. Bring rope and some of the other Brothers at once, we'll put them in the ice house for now with a proper guard."

Again, from the phone, there was some muffled speaking.

The Abbot shrugged. "I was thinking we could experiment on them for a bit. I'm quite keen to see if the grail could restore severed limbs, smashed teeth and broken bones. Ultimately we can do an extensive mind wipe on them; about five years should do it, and we send them on their way. Anyway, we can decide on that later."

He then put the receiver back down on the cradle of the phone, momentarily looking down as he did so.

That was all the opportunity the Guardians needed.

Independently The Wasp and Miss Owl threw the torches they were still holding at the Abbot as hard as they could.

The first torch hit the Abbot's gun, knocking it clean out of his hands, while the second torch hit him just above the eye, making him step back. Seeing his chance, Firefly launched himself forward over the desk and grabbed the Abbot, so he could not retrieve his gun.

"Good work!" cried The Wasp to Firefly and Blue Bolt.

"Thanks," replied Firefly and, nodding down towards the Abbot, asked, "what do we do with him?"

"I've an idea," said The Wasp. "Quick Danni, the grail."

She nodded and went to the open safe where she took the grail from it and moved away.

The Wasp moved over to them and then, taking the Abbot, guided him towards the safe where, taking the excess of the tie cord belt, he threw it inside and slammed the door shut on it. "There," he said, "that should hold for a while."

"You think you'll be able to get away with this?" hissed the Abbot. "Remember I've already summoned help. When I get out of this …"

"Oh, shut up!" cried Blue Bolt as he rammed his cotton handkerchief into the Abbot's mouth to silence him. "C'mon lets go."

And with that the group made for the door and back out into the small corridor. The Wasp was last to leave and, as he did so, he glanced back to the Abbot to see that he was now reaching to the desk trying to grab a letter opener sword which he would use to cut the cord that trapped him. With no time to do anything, The Wasp quickly slammed the door behind him and called a warning to the others that the Abbot would soon be free and to get out as fast as they could.

The small group hastily made their way onto the main landing and to the large staircase which they started to descend.

"To the front door!" cried Miss Owl, noticing with her super sharp eyesight that the key to it was hanging up by the frame on a hook.

By now they had reached the hallway and, taking the lead, Miss Owl made for the main door and grabbed the key, but in her haste dropped it on the floor. Firefly stooped down to pick it up and placed the key in the lock and turned it. He was just about to open the door when a shot rang out, the bullet thumping into the door fame just above his head making them all stop.

"Don't even think about trying to escape," cried the Abbot, as he ran down the stairs, stopping in the hallway, his gun trained on them the whole time. At that point the Dean and several other Monks appeared from a side corridor.

The Abbot called over to the newcomers. "Get them!"

With the order given the Dean and the Monks started to approach the Guardians.

"This is going to be our only chance to get away," prompted The Wasp.

The rest of the group nodded in agreement.

Firefly quickly grabbed the key from the lock and then the handle, opening the door and holding it open for the rest of his friends as they ran through. He then went through himself and started to close the door behind him, aiming to lock it once it was closed, but the Dean got their first and wrenched the door open and successfully made a grab for the key, snatching it out of Firefly's hand. With no other option, Firefly lunged forward and pushed the Dean backwards, making him fall over, blocking the doorway. He then turned and ran after his friends running over the large green lawn towards the avenue of trees that would lead them to the road, The Wasp's car and ultimately freedom.

Then a single gunshot rang out.

Firefly, who of course was behind the small fleeing party, was the target.

The bullet entered his back, passed straight through his body and exploded out of his chest.

He was dead before he hit the ground.

Instinctively, the rest of the Guardians and Danni went straight to their fallen comrade, but it was clear from the terrible wound and his limp body and lifeless expression that stared out at them when they turned him over, he was lost.

"Keep where you are and don't try anything or I'll take another one of you out!"

Everyone turned to see the Abbot marching forward pointing his gun at them. Behind him were the Dean and the other Monks.

"You killed him!" cried Miss Owl in despair, "you murderer!"

"Hardly a major issue considering the present circumstances is it?" replied the Abbot dismissively, stopping a few feet away. He turned to Danni. "Revive him."

"I need water," she replied.

"I've got some here," said Miss Owl as she went to her utility belt and produced her water bottle. Quickly removing the cap she tipped some of the liquid into the grail. Danni held the grail tightly in both hands and spoke softly in ancient Aramaic and it started to glow. First she poured half of the liquid over the wound on Firefly's chest which instantly started to heal. She motioned to the others to turn him over, which they did. Then she poured the remainder of the water onto his back which also started to heal. Seeing the grail was now empty Miss Owl reached forward and tipped some more water into it. With another nod, Firefly was again turned over onto his back and Danni then tipped it over Firefly's mouth. His lips started to move and he instinctively drank the water, he coughed, opening his eyes and slowly sat up. "What happened?" he asked. "Something hit me." He then looked down to see that the front of his costume now had a red stained hole in it.

"You got lucky," chimed in the Abbot, "I killed you and the Grail brought you back, now get to your feet the lot of you!"

CHAPTER 14

Slowly the group stood up, with Danni and Miss Owl helping the still slightly confused Firefly to his feet.

"Seize them!" cried the Abbot to the Monks.

However, before they could make their move, through the air came the faint sound of chanting which slowly started to get louder and louder. Then all around them a green mist started to appear; seemingly seeping up from the ground itself.

"What are you doing?" cried the Abbot in alarm, looking to Danni.

"This is not me!" she protested.

By now the green mist started to take shape into columns and arches, until the small group found themselves in the middle of a large ghostly Quadrangle. From beyond this square, walls, roofs, towers and spires continued to form.

"It's the original Friary building!" cried Danni, looking around.

"In ghostly form," observed The Wasp, as he watched it continuing to take shape.

"Stop this at once," cried the Abbot.

Danni looked at the Abbot and shrugged, whatever was happening was totally out of her control.

"Right, take the grail from her!" ordered the Abbot.

The Dean dutifully ran forward and took it but, as he did so, the cup started to glow and the flesh on his hand instantly started to wither and wilt and, within moments, he was holding the grail in a skeletal hand. He screamed and hurriedly thrust the cup back to Danni before pulling his sleeve up to see that his arm up to the elbow was now just bone.

With the Friary now fully formed the chanting stopped and then, from the arches, appeared a ghostly line of hooded Monks which slowly and menacingly marched over towards them.

"Keep away! Keep away!" cried the Abbot, as he turned and fired his pistol. The bullet passed straight through the Monks in a line and they carried on unharmed.

"Your earthly weapons won't work on us," said the lead figure, as he stopped and pulled back his hood to reveal the ghostly figure of a man in his late sixties.

"Abbot Osborn!" cried Danni in delight. She then turned to the Guardians. "He looked after me in my last years and arranged for me to be buried on the site of St Mary's."

Abbot Osborn smiled. "Yes, I thought you would be safe and undisturbed there, sadly it looks as though I was mistaken."

He turned to face Abbot Morley, staring at him fiercely. "And as for you! How dare you assume my order's name and don our sacred robes."

"I'm, I'm sorry," pleaded the Abbot, glancing over towards the Dean's skeletal arm fearing what could happen to him. He dropped the pistol and threw himself down in front of the ghostly Abbot. "Please don't hurt me, forgive me!"

"Oh, don't worry;" said Abbot Osborn, "there will be time enough for you and your friends to make amends. Now get up."

The Abbot did as he was told.

"Right," said Abbot Osborn, in a business like tone, "it is time to put right what has been undone and make sure the grail and the Damsel are suitably hidden." He then clapped his ghostly hands together. A few moments later, from below, came the sound of a low rumble accompanied moments later by the earth shaking and parting as from it a large stone sarcophagus rose up out of the ground, stopping when it was fully exposed. Then, two of the ghostly monks moved forward to it and between them picked up the lid and stood to one side. From inside the casket, the skeletal occupant stood up and looked around.

"I am afraid, dear brother," said Abbot Osborn apologetically, "that your final resting place is needed by another."

The skeleton turned to look at the Damsel and, understanding the situation and what was required, bowed respectfully, climbed out of the stone casket and moved away across the quadrangle. As he did so he instantly turned to dust, which was carried away on the sudden wind that appeared at that very moment.

"Come my child," prompted Abbot Osborn, "it is time to say your goodbyes."

With a nod, she went to each of the Guardians in turn, thanked them and gave them a hug. She then turned to look at the Abbot, Dean and the rest of the Monks. She smiled and nodded, showing them that she forgave them their actions and that there was no ill feeling towards them.

Then the Damsel carefully climbed inside the sarcophagus and laid down holding the grail across her chest. After a few moments the cup started to glow and the whole casket was filled with light, which quickly faded to reveal that she had returned to her skeletal form. Carefully the two phantoms that were holding the casket's lid replaced it and stood back. Again the ground began to shake and the casket lowered itself back down under the surface of the ground with the disturbed soil and grass repairing itself, leaving no indication that it had ever been broken.

"There," said Abbot Osborn solemnly, "it is done. The Damsel and the grail are again hidden from the world of man. And to that I shall add another form of defence to keep it safe." He turned to Abbot Morley, the Dean and assembled Monks and in a stern voice announced. "You have masqueraded as Monks of the holy Holme for long enough, but no more. From now I decree you are now *truly* members of our sacred order. You shall give up your wicked and illegal ways and lead lives dedicated to others. The weapons you deal in shall all be destroyed and the stolen items you have amassed shall be sold and the proceeds given to those in need. You shall also dedicate yourselves to carrying out good works for the local community and the wider world."

For a moment it looked as though Abbot Morley was going to protest, but he seemed to quickly change his mind and remained silent.

"You shall also do everything within your power to keep this site and the Grail and the

Damsel safe," continued Abbot Osborn.

The Abbot, Dean and the rest of the monks nodded, accepting their new burden.

"And remember," continued Abbot Osborn, "I and those of the order who have passed," he raised his hands to the ghostly monks behind him, "will never be that far away, to help you in times of need or to punish you as required." The last part of the sentence was said with an unmistakable threatening tone. Without waiting for a response the Abbot then turned to the Guardians and, with his tone instantly softening, smiled. "You have done well, all of you."

The group collectively shuffled awkwardly.

"Well," said The Wasp, speaking on the group's behalf, "we only did what was right."

The Abbot smiled. "The Monks of the newly restored Holme order here will now need a link to the outside world. People who can be relied upon to help them if required, would you be prepared to take on that task?"

"Yes, of course," replied The Wasp; while Miss Owl, Firefly and Blue Bolt all nodded.

"Good," said the Abbot, "now that is decided it is time that myself and the rest of my Brothers can return to our slumber." And as he finished speaking he, his ghostly companions, the quadrangle and the rest of the Friary, slowly began to fade, until they all disappeared completely, leaving the Monks and The Guardians standing on the lawn of the Friary.

Eventually it was Miss Owl who broke the silence, speaking to the Dean. "Would you like me to try to take a look at that arm of yours?"

He nodded, looking at his skeletal hand and wiggling the fingers. "Yes, thank you, although I don't think it will do much good."

"Yes," said the Abbot to Miss Owl and the rest of the Guardians, "I think you had all better come inside. It seems we have a lot to discuss …"

EPILOGUE

Lucy rattled the collection of multi sided dice, dropped them down over the game board and then quickly totalled them up. "Thirty points of damage," she announced, with a triumphant smile. "That's the dragon dead!"

"Nope, sorry, I'm afraid not," replied Glenn, who was playing the dragon which was the last obstacle for the team of adventurers to conquer before they had a chance to save the Princess. "You cannot use a *fire attack* on a dragon."

"I can in this case," corrected Lucy quickly. "I'm using a *Shadow Fire attack* on him."

"This dragon is from the Shadow Realm," pointed out Glenn. "He can absorb it and return it straight onto you - so you take the damage, which kills you!"

"You can't do that," grumbled Lucy.

"I can, and I just did," replied Glenn, smiling.

"No way!" exclaimed Lucy.

"Sorry!" replied Glenn. "You're dead!"

"Am not," she protested.

"Hold on! Hold on!" said Carl, as he reached for the game's manual. "Let me look this up, I've no idea who's right on this one."

Just over nine months had passed since The Guardians had entered the graveyard of St Mary's and discovered the body snatching operation.

Under intense police questioning Ron and Ben revealed that they had been stealing skeletons from graveyards up and down the country for the past four years. A special taskforce was created to investigate their crimes and to try and recover the stolen bodies, through the detailed records Ron had kept.

Seizing the opportunity local Archaeologists and Historians insisted on making a full study of the tunnels created under the church. Before they started work Structural Engineers went in to ensure the labyrinth was safe. They soon confirmed it was. However, the four cottages were another matter. After years of neglect in addition to load bearing walls being knocked through, they were quickly condemned and knocked down.

The historical excavations and investigations took nearly six months in total, before the site was turned back over to the church. There was much excitement regarding the finding of a strange chamber with an empty sarcophagus, although they had no idea who could have been buried inside it. This find was only eclipsed by the discovery of a rare 'deviant burial' in an unmarked grave of a man who had had his ribs and jaw removed.

As for the Guardians, their involvement in the grave robbing story and what they were doing to keep the town safe at weekends went global. Not only did it inspire many others to establish their own superhero based groups and go out and help people, but there was also talk of turning their story into a one off drama by one of the TV streaming services. They were even contacted by a special effects team who offered to update and improve their costumes, incorporating wearable tech into them. One addition that Firefly insisted upon adding to his suit was on the chest and back, a red embossed circle with jagged edges. People presumed that it was a red flaming sun, but the reality was it represented the wound he had received when he was briefly killed.

The Guardians did indeed become a link to Holme Friary and the Monks kept their vow to change their ways, even venturing out to help the Guardians with their litter pick and with other charitable events they had planned for the summer and later on at Christmas.

"Okay," announced Carl, after reading the appropriate section in the game's manual, "it looks as though you are *both* technically right, now …"

THUD!

All eyes went to the window where, perched on the sill, was the large headless pigeon. Around his foot was tied a neatly folded piece of paper.

"Ah, looks like Abbot Morley needs our help," observed Glenn.

"Yes, but why, oh why won't he call us on the mobiles?" asked Carl in frustration. "That pigeon has already been spotted and people are asking questions about him!"

"I think someone's made a Facebook group for him," said Will, "and I know I've seen a fan fiction story about him too."

"'Immortal Pigeon'?" asked Carl.

"Yep, that's the one," replied Will, with a nod. "It's pretty good isn't it?"

Lucy rolled her eyes, got up and went over to the window. She opened it, allowing the bird to hop inside. She then carefully took the note from its leg, opened it up and began to read. As she did so, a look of horror spread across her face.

"What is it?" asked Glenn worriedly.

"Abbot Morley has asked us to report to the Friary straight away," replied Lucy, in a shaky voice. "Danni has resurrected herself and the Grail. She says that something is coming, something big, a virus and The Guardians are going to be needed."

AUTHOR'S NOTES

The concept of 'The Guardians' was inspired by two things.

Firstly an organisation called The Street Pastors (as well as a number of independent groups) who do patrol the town centres across the country at the weekends looking after and making sure that people are safe and enjoying themselves. Secondly by the Cos-players (Costume Players) who, apart from attending Science-Fiction Conventions and Comic Cons, also spend their time raising money and taking part in charitable events.

The Superhero characters used in this book are all in the Public Domain. Miss Owl first appeared in Crackajack Funnies #25 (July 1940), The Wasp first appeared in Speed Comics #12 (1941), Firefly Top-Notch #8 (1940) and Blue Bolt first appeared in Blue Bolt Comics vol. 1 #1 (June 1940)

The story of 'The Road to Emmaus' can be found in the New Testament section of the Bible in Luke Chapter 24 Verses 13 - 35.

Printed in Great Britain
by Amazon